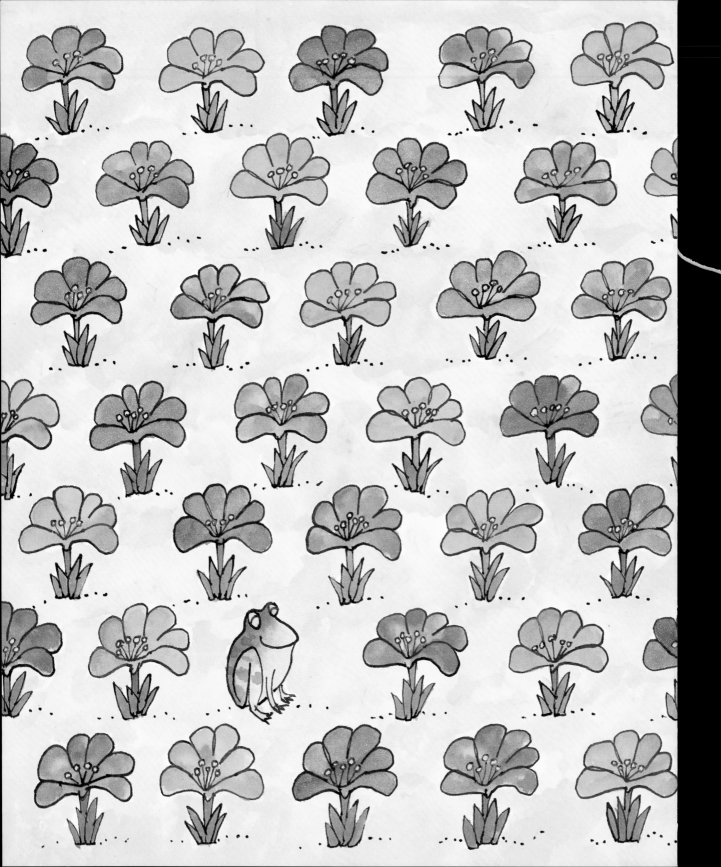

''Pardon?'' Said the Giraffe
First published in England by Walker Books Ltd, London.
Copyright © 1986 by Colin West
Printed in Italy. All rights reserved.
Library of Congress Catalog Card No. 85-45747
ISBN 0-06-443102-9
First Harper Trophy edition, 1986
Published in hardcover by J. B. Lippincott, New York

"PARDON?" SAID THE GIRAFFE

Story and pictures by

Colin West

A Harper Trophy Book

Harper & Row, Publishers

"What's it like up there?"
asked the frog
as he hopped on the ground.

"Pardon?"
said the
giraffe.

"What's it like up there?"
asked the frog
as he hopped on the lion.

"Pardon?"
said the
giraffe.

"What's it like up there?"
asked the frog
as he hopped on the hippo.

"Pardon?"
said the
giraffe.

"What's it like up there?"
asked the frog
as he hopped on the elephant.

"Pardon?" said the giraffe.

"What's it like up there?"
asked the frog
as he hopped on the giraffe.

"It's nice up here, thank you,"
  said the giraffe,
"but you're tickling my nose
  and I think I'm going to…"

"A-A-A-CHOOOOOO

"What's it like down there?"
asked the giraffe.

"Pardon?"
said the
frog.